I'LL MEET YOU AT THE CUCUMBERS

by Lilian Moore

illustrated by Sharon Wooding

ALADDIN PAPERBACKS
New York London Toronto Sydney Singapore

First Aladdin Paperbacks edition June 2001

Text copyright © 1988 by Lilian Moore
Illustrations copyright © 1988 by Sharon Wooding

Aladdin Paperbacks
An imprint of Simon & Schuster
Children's Publishing Division
1230 Avenue of the Americas
New York, NY 10020

Also available in an Atheneum Books for Young Readers hardcover edition.

Typography by Jennifer Dossin.

Printed and bound in the United States of America

10 9 8 7 6 5 4 3

The Library of Congress has cataloged the hardcover edition as follows:

"A Jean Karl book."
Summary: Adam and Junius, two country mice, go for a visit to the city, where Adam despairs when his dear friend admits he might like to stay.
[1. Mice—Fiction. 2. Friendship—Fiction.]
I. Wooding, Sharon, ill.   II. Title.
PZ7.M7865Il 1988 [E] 87–15195
ISBN: 0-689-31243-1 (hc.)

ISBN: 0-689-84496-4 (Aladdin pbk.)

Page 64 constitutes an extension of this copyright page.

CHAPTER

1

"Adam! Adam Mouse! Where are you?"

When Junius Mouse had something important to say he found it hard to wait.

Adam was not in the barn, nor was he under the porch of the farmhouse.

"I'll bet he's thinking again," Junius told himself with a sigh. When Adam was thinking, it was hard to tell him anything.

Junius found Adam sitting comfortably on the old stone wall near the garden.

He waved to Junius. Yes, Adam was thinking aloud again. Junius sat down politely to listen.

"I love this old wall," said Adam.

"See how these stones
trust
one another.
Stone resting on
stone
fitting curve and
edge
together.
Nothing but
stone
on
stone
shaping a wall
against
wind and weather."

"Very true," said Junius. "Listen, Adam. The farmer is going to the city market tomorrow morning. How about coming with me this time?"

Adam shook his head. "It's nice of you to keep asking, Junius. I appreciate it. But I really have no wish to go to the city."

Junius looked at him shrewdly. "Are you afraid of the city, Adam?"

"Afraid?" Adam was offended. "Tell me. Why would anyone want to leave this green and quiet place to go to the city?"

Junius tried again.

"Right next to the Farmer's Market there's a little restaurant. The food crumbs you can pick up! Hot and spicy!" He rolled his eyes. "And they play music on all kinds of horns. Real jazz!" Junius broke into a dance.

"Junius," said Adam patiently. "Go and have a good time."

"I expect to see Amanda Mouse," said Junius. "Any messages?"

"Just give her my regards," said Adam.

Each time the farmer went to the city market, his truck loaded with vegetables, Junius went too. And each time he urged Adam to come along.

Adam had always said no. He liked living in the country, and everything Junius told him about the city sounded rather alarming.

One day Junius had come back with a surprise.

"This is for you," he said, and he had handed Adam a note. "It's from my friend

Amanda. She lives near the market. I told her about you."

Amanda Mouse had written that she would like to be Adam's pen friend. After that Junius carried messages back and forth.

Adam liked Amanda's lively notes. At first he felt shy about writing back. Then he found that if he put down his "thinking aloud" ideas, it was easier. He told her about the smell of fresh-cut hay, about the way he liked to look out of his mouse hole and watch clouds riding across the sky. Things like that.

Usually, when Junius asked Adam to go with him to the city, Adam simply said no.

This time he was troubled.

Junius had asked him if he was afraid. Was he? Was he afraid of new places? Was he just a stick-in-the-mud, without any sense of adventure? Did Amanda like hot and spicy food crumbs, too?

The next morning he watched Junius scamper happily into the farmer's truck.

Junius waved to him. Adam waved back.

Adam Mouse felt troubled and he did not know why.

CHAPTER
2

Adam was very much an outdoor fellow. He had chosen to make his mouse house in the field, right beside the farmer's vegetable garden. It was a simple home, lined with soft grass, with an excellent view of the outside world. Most important, it was easy to get into quickly. Adam Mouse was small and the Enemy was everywhere.

It was delicious to live next to the garden. Peas, lettuce, beet-tops—there was always something to nibble.

Adam sat thinking about the garden. It seemed remarkable to him that so many tasty things could grow so quietly.

No radish ever makes a racket, he thought. Carrots never chatter. Peppers don't prattle.

Aloud, he said:

> "Row on row,
> you never hear the garden
> grow.
>
> Seeds split.
> Roots shove and reach.
> Earth heaves.
>
> Leaves unfurl.
> Stems pierce the
> ground.
>
> Peapods fatten.
> Vines
> stretch and curl.
>
> Such growing
> going on
> without a sound!"

All that thinking about the garden made Adam hungry. He slipped through the little tunnel from his mouse house to the garden and came out right beside a crisp head of lettuce.

With a bit of the lettuce and a snip of carrot and the new small shoot of a spring onion, he made himself a crunchy salad.

My, this is good! Adam thought with relish. Suddenly he found himself wondering what strange crumbs Junius was gorging upon in the city.

After he had eaten, Adam did not hurry back to his mouse house as he usually liked to do. He wandered around the garden, feeling strangely restless.

In the middle of the garden stood the scarecrow the farmer had put up a few days ago. The scarecrow was dressed in old jeans and a work shirt, but he had a dashing red scarf around his neck and a jaunty wide-brimmed hat on his straw head.

What a tall fellow he is! thought Adam. I wonder what the world looks like from way up there?

Adam could never explain to himself what happened next. Surely he knew he was safest on the ground, where he could hide quickly or scurry home.

Yet he ran to the scarecrow and began climbing up.

If he had stopped for an instant, if he had looked up or down, he would have been too frightened to move. Instead, he climbed as fast as he could until he reached the scarecrow's shirt pocket. He jumped into the pocket, panting—his heart pounding.

He sat very still. What if the Enemy-With-Needle-Eyes came swooping out of the sky?

Very carefully, his heart still beating fast, Adam peered out of the pocket, and looked around.

The sun was setting and the sky was rosy with leftover light. Dazzled, Adam watched as the color changed and slowly faded. The sky grew pearly, and suddenly a star appeared.

One star shining in all that sky! Adam thought with pleasure. He had never felt so close to a star before.

After a while, he stretched a wee bit and looked down. At first he thought two small stars had tumbled out of the sky. Then he realized that what he saw were two headlights. The farmer's truck was coming down the road, home from the city.

Junius was back.

Carefully, Adam climbed out of the scarecrow's shirt pocket and made his way back to the ground.

Adam Mouse was already at the truck when Junius jumped out.

"Hi, Adam," he said. "How did you get here so fast?"

"I saw the truck coming down the road," Adam explained.

Junius looked puzzled, so Adam went on in the most casual voice he could manage. "I happened to be sitting way up in the scarecrow's shirt pocket. . . ."

Junius was horrified.

"You climbed the scarecrow?" he cried. "Adam, don't you know how dangerous that is?"

"Yes," said Adam. He liked the way Junius was looking at him. "But the view up there is really superb."

Junius was still shaking his head when he suddenly remembered something.

"Here," he said. He handed Adam a note. "This is for you."

Adam read it quickly. Then he said, "Listen to this, Junius."

"Dear Adam,
    Please come to the city with Junius next week. It would make me so happy if you were here on my birthday.
    Come with Junius to the Farmer's Market.
                    Please!
                        Your pen friend,
                        Amanda Mouse
P.S. I'll meet you at the cucumbers."

"Well, Adam," said Junius, not very hopefully. "What will you do?"

It was hard to tell who was the more surprised when Adam said, "I'm going to the city with you next week!"

CHAPTER
3

Tomorrow, thought Adam.

Junius had said they would be going tomorrow.

For several days Adam had tried to put the trip out of his mind.

Now he sat under the young apple tree that was such a special place. It was early morning, the sweet cool beginning of a summer day. The air smelled lightly of hay and the dew on the grass made tiny flashing rainbows. Adam leaned back with a sigh of pleasure.

"Is it true, Adam Mouse?" Chipmunk

called from a branch on the apple tree. "Is it true?"

Chipmunk leaped from the tree and ran to Adam. "Is it true you are going away?"

Adam sat up, exasperated. Trust Chipmunk to know everything and to get most of it wrong. Chipmunk climbed endlessly from ground to tree and back, collecting nuts and berries and—most eagerly of all, thought Adam—juicy bits of news.

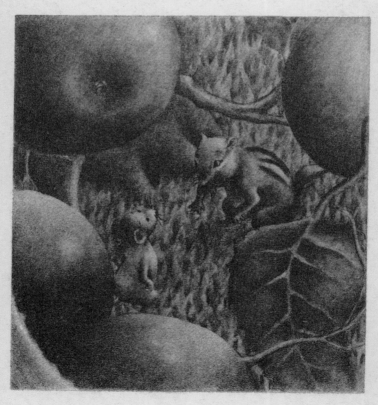

Now Chipmunk stood looking at Adam, his black eyes bright with curiosity, his cheek pouches stuffed with weed seeds.

"I'm just going to the city," Adam explained. "Just for a brief visit."

"The city!" Chipmunk cried in horror, his cheeks bulging and quivering. "Did you hear about Squirrel's cousin? He went to the city and never came back! They say he jumped into a car that was parked here and they drove off and—"

"Excuse me!" Adam said hastily. "I have to find Junius."

He ran very quickly to find his friend, and he was still trembling when he saw Junius near the garden.

"What's the matter, Adam?" said Junius. "Are you all right?"

Adam took a deep breath and put the squirrel-who-never-came-back-from-the-city out of his mind. Here was Junius who always came back. Adam looked at him fondly.

"I'm fine," he said. "What do we do tomorrow?"

"Off we go in the early morn!" Junius sang jubilantly.

"Here's the plan," he went on. "The farmer leaves about sunrise. He packs his crates with vegetables and then loads them onto the truck. While the crates are being loaded, we hide in the last one. Once we're on the truck, we make it to a nice little hay hill I've got fixed up for a soft ride. How about that?"

Junius's excitement was catching.

"Shall I bring some lunch?" asked Adam. "I've got some cheddar-cheese crumbs."

"Good idea," said Junius. "It really wouldn't be safe to eat the farmer's stuff."

"And it wouldn't be honorable," said Adam.

They agreed to meet at the truck at sunrise.

All the way back to his mouse house, Adam thought about a birthday present for Amanda.

What could he give her?

Something from the country, yes.

But what would she like?

Adam had no idea.

Then it will have to be something I like, he decided.

18

That was no problem. Adam knew what he liked best. And he knew just where to find it.

When he got home, he took the present from its special place in his mouse house.

Now to wrap it, he thought. It had to look just right, so Adam hunted until he found a bit of cotton fluff and a bright red thread. Then he packed the gift carefully.

It needed one more thing.

So he wrote it.

CHAPTER
4

The plan worked just as Junius had said it would, and here they were, settled snugly on the little hay hill, waiting for the farmer to take off. Adam had been a little nervous, no denying that. Not Junius, of course. He was an experienced traveler.

"Those cheese crumbs you brought smell good, Adam," said Junius. "Let's have lunch now!"

Adam discovered he was hungry too, so they sat comfortably in the hay, nibbling the cheese. It was interesting to have lunch before breakfast. His big adventure, thought Adam happily, was starting just like a picnic.

Soon they heard the farmer climb into his seat and slam the door of the truck. With a groan and a shudder, the truck began to move.

Adam found that if he stood up and stretched, he could see through some slats in the side of the truck.

I'll stand here all the way, he told himself. Then I won't miss a thing!

The truck bumped and bounced from time to time as it rolled along, and Adam found it a little hard to keep his balance. He had to stand up on his toes now to see through the slats.

He was surprised to see they were passing some farms. It hadn't occurred to him that there were other farms. It made the world seem even larger.

Soon he began to see other trucks on the road.

"Junius," he called. "All these trucks. Are they going to the market, too?"

There was no answer.

Adam turned to look.

Junius was fast asleep.

How can he sleep with all this going on? thought Adam.

At that moment, the truck stopped suddenly, and Adam tumbled back onto the hay.

It was good to sit down after all that standing and stretching. Just for a moment, of course. He didn't want to miss a thing.

The truck began to move again, its wheels humming steadily. Hum. Hum. Hum.

The next thing Adam heard was Junius saying, "Wake up, Adam! We're coming to the big bridge!"

Adam opened his eyes, wondering where he was. Then he jumped up and stood beside Junius, peering eagerly through the slats.

There in the distance was the most magical thing he had ever seen—a great shining web hanging in the air.

"That's the big bridge," said Junius. "Neat, isn't it? We have to cross it to go over the river."

"The river? Is it like our stream?" Adam loved the brook that ran by the farm. Just last night he had watched it flowing silver under the full moon.

"Not exactly," said Junius.

As they approached the bridge, the shining web in the distance became even more magical—pinned to the ground, free in the air, yet sturdy enough for their truck now to ride upon it.

And below the bridge was the river.

Suddenly the world seemed to be nothing but water and sky.

Adam stared in delight at the river.

After a while he said, "Look, Junius! It's a sky mirror!"

> "The cloud
> in the sky is
> the cloud
> in the river.
>
> The sky's
> blueness
> lies there
> too.
>
> Tonight
> the river will
> receive a white
> moon.

The sky is the
giver of
light
to the river."

Junius looked down at the river again.

"You do make a fellow look twice, Adam," he said, nodding.

All too soon for Adam, they had crossed the bridge.

"We're coming into the city!" cried Junius.

Adam could feel his friend's growing excitement.

Junius does love coming here, he thought with a sudden pang.

The truck was moving very slowly, and it seemed to Adam that now they were riding through a great tunnel of sound, under a huge wave of rumbles and roars.

He covered his ears, but the roaring went on.

"Don't worry," Junius told him. "It's just that we're coming into the city and the traffic gets a little heavy here."

The voice of the city, said Adam to himself, is thunder.

C H A P T E R
5

Soon, the truck turned a corner onto a quiet street.

Now Adam could think. He wanted to think about cucumbers. He had never met anybody at a cucumber before. It had never seemed a good idea to stand under a cucumber vine, where most of the cucumbers growing were bigger than he was.

"Adam," said Junius, "there's something I want to tell you."

"Yes?" Adam was still pondering the matter of cucumbers.

"I've been thinking," said Junius, "that I might decide to stay here in the city."

"Not go home?" Adam stared at Junius in astonishment.

"Oh, I'd come back and visit you and the old homestead. But I have a friend here— Orlando Mouse—who says I can share his house, and I'm trying to make up my mind. It's a very tempting offer."

Adam sat very still. What was it Chipmunk had said? *He went to the city and never came back.*

Junius saw Adam's stricken face.

"Now don't you worry, Adam," he said. "If I decide to stay, I'll see that you get back on the truck safely."

He doesn't understand, thought Adam. Suddenly he felt a great loneliness and wished he were back in his little mouse house in the field.

The truck pulled to a stop, and Junius cried happily, "Here we are, Adam. Just stay close and follow me!"

Adam never quite remembered how they left the truck, or how they made their way along the boxes on the ground to the cucumber stand.

All he felt as he followed his friend was a great hollow sadness in his chest.

Junius led Adam into a little tunnel.

"This takes us to a snug burrow right under the cucumber stand," Junius explained.

Adam was still so shaken by what Junius had told him that he hardly heard him now.

"That's where we're meeting Amanda," said Junius as they ran along.

Amanda!

I really have to pull myself together, thought Adam.

They soon reached the little burrow. It was indeed snug—and there was his pen friend, Amanda Mouse.

Adam found himself looking at the most welcoming smile he had ever seen.

"I'm so glad you could come," said Amanda.

She really seems glad to see me, thought Adam. Shyly, he said, "Thank you."

Then to his dismay, he heard Junius say,

"Amanda, do you mind showing Adam the sights? I've got something *very* important to take care of. I'll catch up with you at your place soon. OK?"

What was the matter with Junius? Why was he running off like this? What was so important?

With unruffled good humor, Amanda said, "We'll see you later then, Junius," and waved as he left.

She seemed to read Adam's thoughts. "Junius gets a bit excited when he comes to the city," she told him. "Don't worry. He'll find us."

As soon as Junius had gone, Adam was overcome again with shyness.

Suddenly he remembered the gift he had brought.

"Happy birthday!" he said, and thrust the package at Amanda.

"Why, thank you, Adam," said Amanda.

"There's a note with it," said Adam. "It's a kind of riddle."

Amanda unfolded the note on the package and read it aloud:

"I come from the heart of
a flower.
Among many, I was one.
I have a secret power, and
I bring you the taste of the sun."

"Adam," said Amanda. "Would you think I was awful if I opened it this very minute? I can't wait!"

"Neither can I," said Adam, truthfully.

Eagerly, Amanda unwrapped the package.

"Oh my!" she said. There lay the largest, fattest sunflower seed she had ever seen.

"My favorite food!" she cried. "Wherever did you get one like this?"

"It dropped from a sunflower in the farmer's garden," Adam told her. "One of many seeds that fell. The flower grew on a stalk taller than a man!"

Wide-eyed, Amanda cried, "Taller than a man!"

"With a huge head, filled with seeds," Adam went on, remembering the great sunflower, "and it always turned to the sun. In the morning, you know, the sunflower turns to the east. It follows the sun across the sky, and ends the day turned to the west, where the sun goes down."

Amanda was still gazing in wonder at the fat sunflower seed.

"And what is its secret power?" she asked.

Adam laughed. "Well, if we planted it, it might grow to be a sunflower taller than a man. . . ."

"Oh!" said Amanda, astonished.

"But if you eat it," Adam said, "you might taste the sun."

"Let's eat it, right now," Amanda decided. "It looks scrumptious. Let's share it."

"No, no!" cried Adam. "It's for you!"

"It will be more fun if we share," said Amanda.

It was very hard for Adam to resist. As a matter of fact, it was impossible. So they shared the sweet, delicious sunflower seed.

It did indeed taste of the sun.

CHAPTER

6

"Adam," said Amanda. "Would you like to see where I live?"

"To tell the truth," Adam replied, "I'm very curious."

"It's not far," Amanda told him. "But we have to be careful getting out of here. Come this way."

They ran out of the burrow onto a low wall. Suddenly Adam stopped.

"What is it?" asked Amanda. "What's wrong?"

"Look! Up there! Look at that great red jewel in the sky!"

"Adam," Amanda said gently. "That's a traffic light." The red jewel disappeared. Now a bright emerald seemed to be hanging in the air.

"It's beautiful!" Adam whispered. "Why did it change its color?"

"It keeps changing from red to green," Amanda explained. "When the light is red, people and cars have to stop. When the light turns green, they can go."

"What a clever idea!" Adam marveled. "Who ever thought of that?"

He would have stood rooted there watching the changing of the light, but Amanda hurried him on.

"It's not safe here," she told him. "We lost a dear friend here last week."

Adam shivered, even as he admired the steadiness of Amanda's voice.

"I live across the street, but we don't have to wait for the traffic light," she said with a laugh. "We'll cross under the street."

With a last look at the emerald glowing in the sky, Adam followed Amanda into a dark hole.

* * *

Adam felt as if they had left the real world behind—the world of sky and light and warmth.

Here all was darkness and dankness and mysterious noises. They were walking on great metal pipes that lay crisscrossed like streets, cold and hard to walk on. His feet hurt—how different this was from the grassy fields of home—and he hoped Amanda couldn't hear how loudly his heart was beating.

He jumped at a sudden explosion of sound in the distance.

"That's just a faraway subway," Amanda reassured him. "That's a train that runs under the streets."

Trains under the streets! The voice of the city is thunder, thought Adam, above the streets and under.

Several times they had to stop abruptly and stand very still as great dark shadows darted past.

"Those are rats," Amanda said. "A part of the family I'm not very fond of!"

At last they emerged into the light.

"This is the basement of the house I live in," said Amanda. "We can climb right up this wall to my place."

Adam was a good climber, but he was a little surprised to see what a fast and sturdy climber Amanda was.

He just about managed to stay right behind her until they reached the hole that led into her house.

"Here we are!" said Amanda.

Adam looked around with interest.

On the walls, bits of colored paper made lively designs. On the floor, piles of soft shredded yarn made bright little rugs.

A small red woolen sock lay neatly in one corner.

"That's my new sleeping bag," Amanda explained.

Puzzled, Adam asked, "Where did you get such unusual furnishings?"

Amanda laughed. "I live next door to a small boy's room. Come and look."

Peering through the hole in the wall, Adam could see right into the boy's room.

"Messy, isn't it?" said Amanda. "But it's full of treasures."

"Doesn't he mind if you take something?"

"He likes me. Sometimes he sits watching this hole, hoping to see me. Yesterday he left me a piece of his peanut butter sandwich. Let's go in and look around."

Adam drew back, alarmed.

"Don't worry," said Amanda. "He's still at school."

The boy's room was indeed full of treasures.

"He must like to build things," said Adam,

"and color things—

and read—

and, my goodness, he must like to play ball!"

"Look at this, Adam," said Amanda, pointing to a little silver automobile. "This is my very favorite thing in here."

She hopped into the car, pressed a little lever, and began zooming around the room.

Adam watched, overcome with admiration.

Amanda pulled up beside Adam and got out of the car.

"Would you like to take it for a spin?" she asked.

Adam was torn between fear and longing.

Maybe it would be fun just to sit in the shiny silver car. He got in.

"Press this to make it go," said Amanda. "Press lightly to go slowly. Press harder to pick up speed. Hold on to the steering wheel and turn it the way you want to go."

She smiled at Adam, encouragingly.

Cautiously, he touched the lever. The car began to move. He pressed a little harder and the car went faster. Suddenly, Adam felt as if he could do anything. He pressed the lever all the way down and the car began to speed around the room. He felt the wind in his face as he went faster and faster.

"I'm driving a car!" he exulted. "Here I am driving a car!"

He went around and around as if he never wanted to stop. Then he saw Amanda beckoning him.

He pulled up beside her. "I think we'd better go now," she said.

With a loving last look at the little car, Adam followed Amanda back through the hole to her place.

"I think you should know," said Amanda. "You just drove the Silver Racer!"

CHAPTER 7

"I have some of the peanut butter sandwich left," said Amanda. "Let's share it."

Adam was still aglow with the feeling that he could try anything. As he began to nibble the peanut butter bits, he found them rather tasty. Suddenly his mouth stuck together, and for an awful moment it seemed to be permanently stuck. It took some hard chewing to pry his mouth open. He hoped Amanda didn't notice the strange faces he was making.

Amanda, however, had walked over to a space in the wall where she kept special things.

"Look," she said to Adam. "I have all the letters you sent with Junius. I like to reread them." She held one up. "But I don't quite understand this one."
She read it aloud:

"*The small apple tree
hums
with bee buzz,
with the beat of bee wings.*

It's Spring.

The small tree
hums and
sings

of apples in the fall."

"Amanda," said Adam, "do you know where apples come from?"

"Why, yes," she replied. "In boxes. I've seen them."

"They may end up in boxes," Adam told her. "But they grow on trees."

He thought of the young tree he so loved to sit under.

"In the spring," he went on, "the apple tree is covered with the nicest pink and white flowers. I don't think there's anything that can make you feel as happy as an apple tree in blossom."

"What's the bee buzz?" Amanda wanted to know.

"The bees love the sweet-tasting blossoms. Sometimes there are so many bees in the apple tree that it sounds as if the tree is singing. Later, the blossoms fall off and the apples begin to grow."

41

"—and end up in boxes in the fall." Amanda laughed.

Then she said thoughtfully, "You know a lot of important things, Adam."

Adam pondered that. "In the country," he said, "you get to know about roots—about where things come from."

"Adam," said Amanda slowly, "I'm ashamed to tell you this, but the very thought of the country scares me. Everything Junius tells me sounds so dangerous!"

Adam was flabbergasted.

"I think of the country," Amanda went on, "as miles and miles of open space. . . ."

"Well, yes," said Adam. "There is open space."

". . . and it all sounds so wild and so . . . so lonely." She shivered as she spoke.

How was he to tell her, thought Adam, what the country was really like? Imagine! She felt safe here in the city, where half the time his heart was in his mouth!

Adam sighed.

"Anyway," he said, "I'm glad you like the thoughts in my letters from the country."

"Thoughts?" said Amanda. "Is that what you call them?"

"Well, it sometimes takes a lot of thinking to say what I feel."

Amanda gave Adam a strange look.

"Thoughts," she repeated.

"Adam," she said, "I have something *very* important to show you. Let's go right now."

"Go where?" asked Adam.

"To the Library."

"For another adventure?" asked Adam.

"Yes," said Amanda. "A very special one."

They ran down the wall to the basement and then into a wide tunnel.

They emerged from the tunnel beside a small and pleasant park.

Adam stopped short with a cry of delight.

"Grass! Trees!" His feet seemed to be yearning to walk on soft earth. "Can we go in there for a little while?"

"The park *is* pretty," said Amanda gravely. "But it's very dangerous. People bring their animals there. This is Enemy territory, Adam."

"Look at that squirrel!" cried Adam. "He's eating right out of someone's hand!" He shook his head in disbelief. "If you came near a squirrel in the country, he'd be up a tree so fast you'd hardly see the tip of his tail!"

"I guess squirrels in the park are city folk," said Amanda.

Adam wondered. Could that squirrel be the one Chipmunk spoke of? The one who never came back? Once he'd learned city ways, did he ever think of home?

What would happen to Junius if he stayed here? Would he become city folk, too?

CHAPTER
8

When they entered the Library, Adam and Amanda found themselves in a cheerful room that held low tables, chairs, and shelves filled with books.

Adam looked around curiously. Then he sniffed. "It has a nice smell."

"It must be the smell of all those words on paper," said Amanda. "I sometimes come here to listen to the Story Hour. Adam, you wouldn't believe how many wonderful stories have been written about us—mice heroes and mice heroines, mice adventurers, mice detectives, mice families. The children love us."

"How do the grown-ups feel?" asked Adam.

"Well, not *exactly* the same," said Amanda.

Amanda was looking for something. She scampered from one table to another. Then she called to Adam, "This is what I want to show you."

Adam ran to the table and hopped up beside her.

"This book," she said. "Help me turn the pages."

Then she watched Adam as he began reading. She watched him silently, turning the pages with him as he went on reading.

"Amanda!" His voice was breathless. "This book is full of thoughts!"

"Adam," said Amanda. "These thoughts are poems, like yours. They are written by poets. And that's what you are, Adam—a poet." She smiled. "My pen friend is a poet who writes me poems!"

"A poet," said Adam, as if he were tasting the word.

"Lots of books on these shelves are books of poems," said Amanda.

Adam looked around, impressed.

"There must be lots of poets then," he said.

Amanda nodded. "Oh, yes. You have company."

"Do people like poets?" asked Adam.

"I don't know," said Amanda. "But they need them."

"Need them?" Adam was puzzled.

"Yes, poets are very helpful."

Amanda was thoughtful for a moment. Then she said, "I think it's the way poets see things—as if everything were new. Then we read the poems and we feel, 'Yes, that's the way it is.' "

By now Adam was impatient to go on reading the poems, so they turned another page.

"Listen to this thought, I mean poem," he cried. "Listen!"

> "*Grass on the lawn*
> *Says nothing:*
> *Clipped, empty,*
> *Quiet.*
>
> *Grass in the fields*
> *Whistles, slides,*
> *Casts up a foam*
> *Of seeds,*

Tangles itself
With leaves: hides
Whole rustling schools
Of mice."

"Oh, Amanda, how true that is! This poet understands grass."

They turned a page, and Adam said, "Just listen to this one!"

"Humps are lumps
and so are mumps.

Bumps make lumps
on heads.

Mushrooms grow
in clumps of lumps—
on clumps of stumps,
in woods and dumps.

Springs spring lumps
in beds.

Mosquito bites
make itchy lumps.

Frogs on logs
make twitchy lumps."

He laughed aloud.

"This poet understands lumps."

"I wish we could stay, so you could read all the poems," said Amanda. "But the children will be coming in here soon. And we do have to get back to meet Junius."

"Just one more," said Adam.

They turned the page and Adam began to read,

> "The fog comes
> on little cat feet—"

"No, not that one!" said Adam, and they turned the page quickly.

"This one," said Adam.

> "I loved my friend
> He went away from me.
> There's nothing more to say,
> The poem ends,
> soft as it began—
> I loved my friend."

And this poet understands how I feel about Junius, he said to himself with a sigh.

CHAPTER
9

"Let's take this shortcut back," said Amanda as she led the way down one wall and through a winding passage.

"You must know every pathway in the city," said Adam as he hurried on behind her.

When they came out into the street, Amanda quickened her pace.

"I do feel safer," she said, "when I'm not right out in the open too long. Don't you feel the same way, Adam?"

There was no answer.

"Adam?"

Amanda stopped and turned around.

Adam was not there.

Amanda stood very still.

Where could he be?

Had he gone back to the children's room? Of course! That was it.

She must get him away before the children came trooping in.

Amanda ran back to the Library and into the children's room.

"Adam!" she called.

There was no reply.

She scampered from corner to corner, from table to table, hoping to catch sight of him.

Adam was not there.

She had to face it. Adam was lost.

How frightened he must be!

She trembled as she thought how she would feel, lost in the countryside with all its unknown terrors.

Had she hurried him too much?

Had he taken a wrong turn?

She went back into the street, retracing her steps, calling his name.

But there was no sign of Adam.

Amanda stood still and thought about what to do next.

She would have to go and get Junius. They would have to organize a search party.

Quickly, she made her way to the tunnel entrance near the park.

Just as she was about to slip into the tunnel, she heard "Amanda!"

There was Adam, sitting outside the park, very much absorbed in something.

Amanda was overwhelmed with relief at the

sight of him. "Oh, Adam!" she cried. "I thought you were lost!"

"I'm so sorry, Amanda," said Adam, "I didn't mean to worry you like that. I just got carried away!" He wrinkled his nose. "What *is* that marvelous smell? It seemed to pull me all the way here."

"A man in the park," said Amanda, "is selling roasted peanuts."

"Roasted peanuts!" Adam took a deep, delicious breath. "What a fantastic smell! Please forgive me, Amanda. I was quite overcome!"

Adam looked so remorseful that Amanda said in a kindly voice, "Yes. I remember the first time I smelled roasted peanuts."

Adam had a lot to think about on the way back. Not often does one smell roasted peanuts. Not every day does one discover that he is a poet, part of a large company of poets. Amanda had said that poets were needed. Adam liked that.

This had certainly been a day of unexpected happenings.

There was one more surprise.

CHAPTER
10

When they ran into the house, Amanda and Adam were greeted with a loud burst of song.

The room was crowded with Amanda's friends, and they were all singing,

"Happy birthday to you,
Happy birthday to you,
Happy birthday, dear Amanda,
Happy birthday to you!"

Amanda gasped. "I never dreamed. . . ." was all she could say. Everyone was delighted. A surprise party has to be a surprise.

There was Junius, laughing.

"Now you know, Adam, why I ran off so fast. I had to get the gang together for this party."

Then Adam was introduced to the others— to Rosa Mouse, to Orlando, to MacGregor Mouse.

Rosa Mouse was small and beautiful. "We've heard so much about you," she said to Adam.

"I'm sure glad to meet Junius's friend," said Orlando heartily.

So this was Orlando who was tempting Junius to stay in the city! Adam tried to dislike him, but he was so merry that it was hard.

MacGregor Mouse was very dignified, a little older than the others. Junius introduced Adam to him, saying proudly, "MacGregor is president of the Regional Mountain Climbing Club."

He, too, said he was happy to meet Adam.

They are all so friendly, thought Adam. They made him feel as if he belonged.

And what food they had all brought for the party! There were fine cheeses—some Brie and imported Swiss cheese—and a great spread of pepperoni pizza.

"Dive in, everybody!" called Orlando.

And everybody did.

Hot spicy crumbs! After his mouth cooled off a bit, Adam thought the pepperoni pizza was delicious.

As they sat around eating, Junius said to MacGregor Mouse, "Tell us about the next climb."

"That's to be the big one," said MacGregor Mouse. "Next Tuesday night, the whole Mountain Climbing Club is going to the Museum to make an assault on the Bone Mountain."

"That's the skeleton of a huge dinosaur in the Museum," Junius explained to Adam. "No mouse has reached the top yet."

"We will this time!" MacGregor said confidently.

"By the way," said Junius, "Adam here is probably the only mouse who's ever climbed a scarecrow."

When Junius had explained what a scarecrow was, everyone was impressed.

"That is certainly a first," said MacGregor.

"Hooray for Adam!" cried Orlando. "Let's make him an honorary member of our Mountain Climbing Club."

"Done!" said MacGregor.

Adam was overwhelmed. The food. The friendship. And now this honor.

"And what's more," Amanda announced to her friends, "Adam is a poet."

"A poet!" cried Rosa. "Oh, Adam, tell us a poem. Please!"

Adam was among friends. So he stood up and said, "Where I live, it is easy to see the sky."

> "I've watched a
> cloud
> nibble
> a slice of moon.
>
> I've seen the sky
> at dusk
> fill
> with spilling sun.
>
> And once
> I saw a star,
> just one
> alone in all that sky."

Everyone was silent for a moment.

"Ah," said MacGregor. "That's part of the joy of climbing, getting to see more sky."

Rosa gave a sigh of pleasure. "Thank you, Adam."

The food had all been eaten by now.

It was getting late.

It was time to go.

"To be safe," said MacGregor Mouse, "we had better leave here one by one." He was the first to leave.

After that, Rosa said good-bye and slipped out.

Then it was Orlando's turn to go.

"Good-bye, Adam," he said. "Good-bye, Junius. Hope I see you next week." And he, too, was gone.

Junius was not going to live with Orlando.

Adam was flooded with happiness.

As calmly as he could, he said to Junius, "What made you decide to go home?"

Junius was thoughtful for a moment. Then he said, "My feet hurt."

Suddenly Adam realized how glad he was to be going home. How much there would be to tell Junius as they sat on the little hay hill in the truck bound for the farm!

It would be hard to say good-bye to Amanda, though.

Again, as if she read Adam's thoughts, she said to him and Junius, "I'd like to go with you to the cucumbers."

So the moment to say good-bye was put off for a little while, until the three had made their way back to the burrow under the cucumber stand.

Then it was truly time to go.

"I'm glad I came for your birthday," said Adam.

"I am, too," said Amanda, smiling.

Suddenly Adam said, "Amanda, would you come for a visit to the country?"

Junius said hurriedly, "Amanda's kind of nervous about our neck of the woods, Adam."

"Because she doesn't know," said Adam. "How about it, Amanda?"

Amanda frowned. "Come out to those miles of open space . . . where it's so wild and lonely?"

"Where you can eat seeds from a sunflower taller than a man," said Adam, "and see ap-

ples on a tree . . . maybe even see a poem grow!
Will you come, Amanda?"

She stood thinking.

Then she smiled.

"Yes," said Amanda. "Yes, I will."

Dear Reader:

You may want to know who wrote the poems that Adam Mouse read in the library.

"Grass" was written by the poet Valerie Worth.

"Lumps" was written by the poet Judith Thurman.

"Poem" was written by the poet Langston Hughes.

This is the poem that Adam Mouse and Amanda Mouse did *not* want to read:

> *The fog comes*
> *on little cat feet.*
>
> *It sits looking*
> *over harbor and city*
> *on silent haunches*
> *and then, moves on.*

It was written by the poet Carl Sandburg.